Douglas & McIntyre Ltd.
585 Bloor Street West
Toronto, Ontario M6G 1K5

Canadian Cataloguing in Publication Data

Klinting, Lars
Beaver the baker
1st Canadian ed.
Translation of: Castor bakar.
ISBN 1-55054-252-4

I. Title.

PZ7.K55Be 1997   j839.73'74   C96-930961-9

Title lettering by Anthony Liliefeldt
Printed in Belgium, 1998

LARS KLINTING

Beaver
the Baker

DOUGLAS & McINTYRE

VANCOUVER / TORONTO

Who's that knocking on Beaver's window?

It's Frippy! He has come to wish Beaver
a happy birthday.

Beaver is very glad to see him. But what can he offer
his friend? Frippy is always so hungry.

We'll make a cake!

This is Beaver's
kitchen. He has lots
of pots and bowls that used
to belong to his grandmother.
She was a good cook.

But what are Beaver and Frippy
looking for?

Grandma's old notebook, of course!
It has the recipe for the best cake.

It's important to read the recipe carefully, and to make sure that you have all the ingredients.

First of all Beaver brings out the butter,
which he melts in a small pan.

Then he takes out
the breadcrumbs,

the pastry
brush

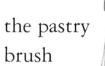

and the baking pan.

Beaver carefully brushes the inside of the baking pan with some of the melted butter.

Then Frippy pours the breadcrumbs into the baking pan. He gently shakes the pan so that the crumbs stick to the butter.

Meanwhile, Beaver turns on the oven.

Beaver takes out

sugar,

eggs

and the old bowl.

(He could really use a new one!)

Beaver breaks the eggs into the bowl.
Frippy adds the sugar.

Now Beaver takes out

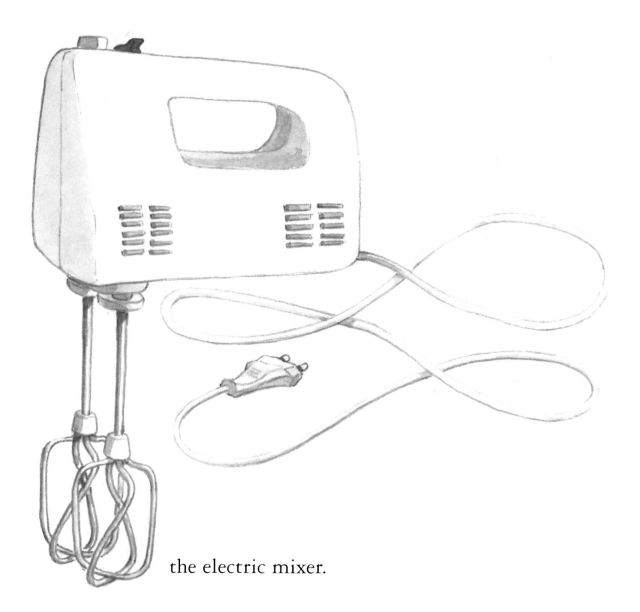

the electric mixer.

He beats the eggs and the sugar for a long time,
until the mixture is fluffy and almost white.

Beaver takes out

the baking soda,   the vanilla   and the flour,

which he stirs together
in a small bowl.

Then Frippy brings the wooden spoon   and the milk.

Beaver pours the milk and the melted butter
into the egg mixture.

Frippy adds the flour mixture from the
small bowl.

Beaver stirs it all together well.

Beaver and Frippy pour the batter into the
baking pan.

There's still a little batter left in the bowl.
Frippy thinks it's delicious!

Now the cake goes into the oven.
Watch out, it's hot!

Beaver's oven has a window, so they can watch
the cake as it bakes.

"Just like TV," says Frippy.

Beaver sets the timer so they'll know when
the cake is ready.

But look at this mess!

They can do the dishes while the cake
is in the oven.

The cake is ready. It has to cool down a bit
before they can turn it onto a plate.

Frippy puts a doily
upside-down on the cake.

Then he puts a plate upside-
down on the doily.

Now comes the tricky part.
Beaver turns the whole thing over
so that the cake pan is on the top.

Abracadabra! Look how nicely
it turned out.

Beaver and Frippy take out

the tablecloth,

the juice,

the glasses,

the plates,

the napkins

and a knife to cut the cake.

They set the table.

But what now? There's a knock on the door.

"Happy birthday to you
Happy birthday to you
Happy birthday, dear Beaver ..."
　"Quick, Frippy!" says Beaver. "More juice
and plates!"

It's a good thing they made the cake! There was just enough for everyone, and it tasted very good.

BEAVER'S CAKE

1/2 cup (125 mL) butter or margarine
2 tbsp (25 mL) plain breadcrumbs
1 cup (250 mL) granulated sugar
2 large eggs
1 1/2 cups (375 mL) all-purpose flour
1 1/2 tsp (7 mL) baking soda
1 tsp (5 mL) vanilla extract
1/2 cup (125 mL) milk

1. Turn on the oven to 350 F (180 C).
2. Melt the butter on low heat.
3. Brush a 9-inch (23 cm) baking pan with a little of the melted butter.
4. Pour the breadcrumbs into the baking pan. Shake the pan carefully so that the crumbs stick to the butter. (It's important to prepare the pan properly so the cake doesn't stick.)
5. Beat the sugar and eggs in a large bowl, preferably with an electric mixer, until the mixture is white and fluffy.
6. Combine the flour and baking soda in a separate bowl. Stir it together very well. (Make sure there are no lumps!) Then stir it into the egg mixture.
7. Add the vanilla, milk and the rest of the melted butter to the egg mixture. Blend it in very well.
8. Pour the batter into the baking pan. Bake the cake for about 35 minutes. (Stick a toothpick or knife into the middle of the cake. If it comes out clean, the cake is done!) When the cake has cooled a little, turn it out onto a serving plate. If you like, sift a little icing sugar on top of the cake.